JUST jaime

JUST Jaime

TERRI LIBENSON

BALZER + BRAY
An Imprint of HarperCollins*Publishers*

Balzer + Bray is an imprint of HarperCollins Publishers.

Just Jaime

www.harpercollinschildrens.com

Library of Congress Control Number: 2018968544
ISBN 978-0-06-285107-9 (trade ed.) — ISBN 978-0-06-285106-2 (pbk.)
ISBN 978-0-06-291530-6 (special ed.) — ISBN 978-0-06-291619-8 (special ed.)
ISBN 978-0-06-291549-8 (special ed.) — ISBN 978-0-06-293749-0 (special ed.)

Typography by Terri Libenson and Katie Fitch
19 20 21 22 23 PC/LSCC 10 9 8 7
❖
First Edition

To my kids, who navigated middle school drama
with so much grace. You could've taught me a thing or two.

PROLOGUE: JAIME

You always think bad things are gonna happen to somebody else, not you.

But then they do, and BOOM. Your world turns upside down. And it's really physical stuff, let me tell you.

First, you get that pins-and-needles feeling all over.

Then your stomach falls to your feet.

Then you freeze.

And finally, all the emotions come flooding in—your heart pounds and you get the shakes.

I've gotta admit, I'd never experienced it before. And I never want to again. I think it's that fight-or-flight thing we learned about in science. Ms. Flancher told us all about these hormones that rush from some gland in your nervous system. I was half paying attention. Because, as I said, I never thought it would happen to me.

Good thing is I know my system works. Bad thing is neither my body or brain knows what it wants to do:

take flight . . .

. . . or fight.

JAIME

It's the last day of school. I need to get ready, but I can't decide what to wear. I'm standing in front of my closet, and nothing is jumping out at me. Everything looks so babyish.

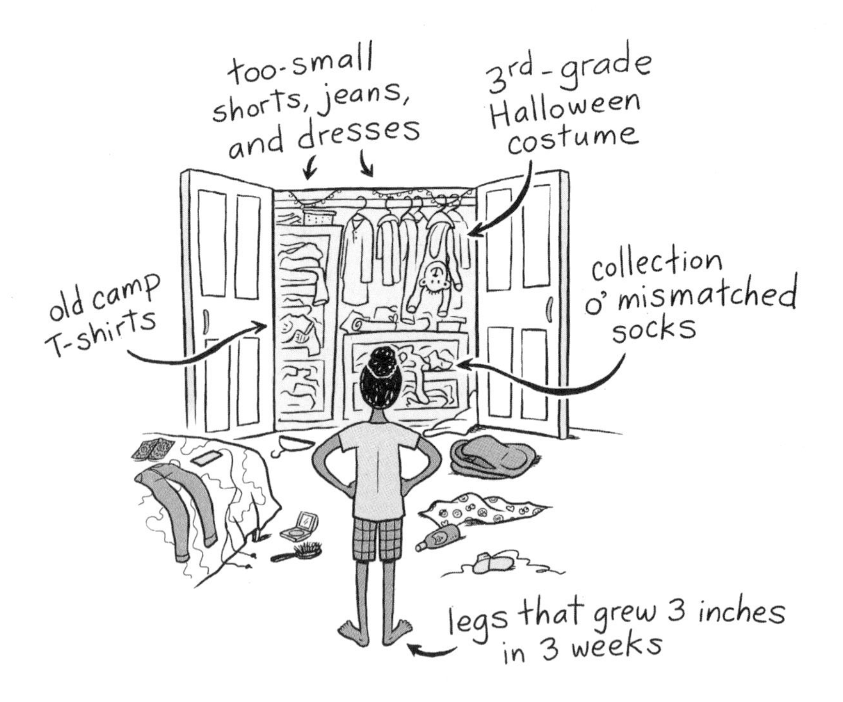

I need something perfect. Not for me, not for boys, and not even for the last day of school. I just need to look cool, confident, and mature.

It's mainly 'cause I have to talk to Maya once and for all. We could really use a friendship do-over. Especially for summer.

Summer. I'm sooo ready.

Well, on one hand I am. On the other . . .

Okay, here's the thing. For the past few months, weird stuff has been happening. Like, alien weird.

Yeah, I **wish** I could blame aliens.

Sometimes my friends are super nice to me, and other times it feels like they're a million miles away. Sometimes they pretend they don't hear me, and sometimes they **tease** me for things I say or do.

This has been happening more and more, and I don't know why. Everything was fine in sixth grade and most of seventh.

For a while, I thought I was imagining it. In fact, whenever I'd bring it up, they'd tell me it's all in my head and accuse me of being too sensitive. And that when they tease me, they're only kidding, and that's what friends do.

Their kidding isn't very friendly, though.

Lately, I've tried to shove my feelings down and pretend everything is okay. But I've reached a breaking point. It's officially summer tomorrow. I don't want to feel ignored at the pool or teased for looking like a baby in my bikini.

So today, I've decided to talk to Maya about it, once and for all. She's my best friend. Yeah she's been acting strange, but underneath she's a good person, and she'll tell me the truth. I want to know why she's been distant, why Celia runs hot and cold, and why Grace always kisses Celia's butt.

I also want to figure everything out soon, because I **just** don't want it to be weird. I want to have fun on my last day of seventh grade!

So yeah, that's my plan. Talk to Maya and get my life settled by third period, before we're dismissed for Field Day. It's time.

Now if only I could find something to wear.

Maya

I'M STARING AT THE CEILING. IT HAS A LOT GOING ON.
horsefly crawling
ceiling fan
old stickers from first grade
bugs trapped in glass bulb
deflated balloons from January birthday
crack shaped like jellyfish
stain from old body spray explosion (also shaped like jellyfish)

I STARE 'CAUSE I'D RATHER LIE HERE THAN GET UP. I HAVE TO DO SOMETHING THAT I'M TOTALLY DREADING.
paralyzed
fly on the loose
I KNOW IT'S THE RIGHT THING TO DO, BUT HECK — I DON'T WANT TO BE THE BAD GUY. I'M *NEVER* THE BAD GUY. WHAT I REALLY NEED IS A PLAN.
PLAN A: Go through with it, no looking back.
PLAN B: Disguise self and blow town.

I HEAR MY NAME. AT FIRST, I THINK SOME HIGHER POWER IS MOTIVATING ME, BUT IT'S JUST MY MOM. MUST BE GETTING LATE.
MAYA!
God?
MAYA!
I FORCE MYSELF OUT OF BED AND GET READY SUPER FAST.
It's for the best, it's for the best....
kitchen
"Dora the Explorer" on repeat
Backpack, Backpack, Backpack, I'm the BACKPACK!

MY BABY SISTER IS HOGGING THE CEREAL... *AND* THE TV.
shoving stale banana muffin in mouth
mom
little sister, Lily, 2½
weirdly large head
"MAP! MAP!"
fun fact: mom cut my hair like Dora's before she took me to a real salon
I still hide the photos
nom
nom
PoP! Sugar O's
MY KID SISTER IS CUTE (BIG HEAD AND ALL), BUT SHE'S A HANDFUL. I'M 10½ YEARS OLDER THAN LILY. JAIME THINKS SHE WAS MY PARENTS' LAST-DITCH EFFORT AT HAPPINESS BEFORE THE DIVORCE.
dump
well, she's comic relief, anyway

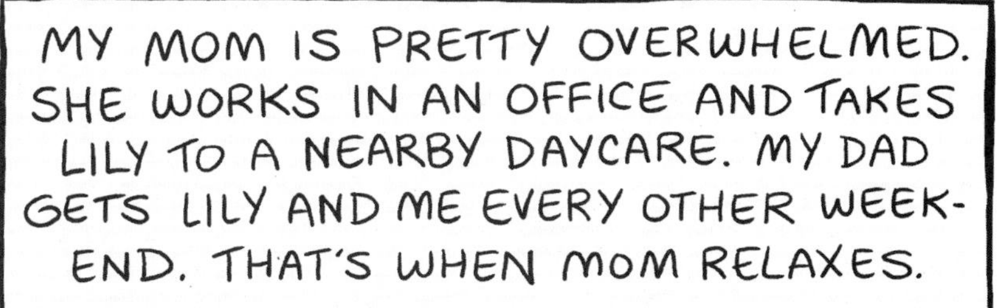
MY MOM IS PRETTY OVERWHELMED. SHE WORKS IN AN OFFICE AND TAKES LILY TO A NEARBY DAYCARE. MY DAD GETS LILY AND ME EVERY OTHER WEEK-END. THAT'S WHEN MOM RELAXES.

She once stayed in the bathtub an entire weekend
So pruny, she looked 150 when she got out
bubble

MY MOM LOWERS THE VOLUME AND WIPES LILY'S STICKY MOUTH.
So, kiddo, all set for the last da— oh shoot, where's her sippy cup?
sippy cup
YUM, DELICIOSO!
I guess. Got a headache.

Are you and Jaime going to the pool later?
Dunno. Might just be me an' the others.
wipe wipe
Seriously? I haven't seen Jaime in a while. You two okay?
Yeah. She's just busy. Last week of school an' stuff.
I DON'T TELL HER THE TRUTH. HOW CAN I? MOM'S KNOWN JAIME SINCE WE WERE IN KINDERGARTEN.
Jai and me as Kindergartners
ONLY THING IS, I'M A DIFFERENT PERSON NOW. EVEN CELIA AND GRACE AGREE.
Jai and me now
(not changed much)

LILY GRABS A CHUNK OF MOM'S HAIR TO GET HER ATTENTION. IT WORKS.
Aaack, Lily. Maya, honey, you'd better get a move on. Whoa, is that the time?
spill-proof cup
MAP!
I got it.
No, no, go ahead. You're going to be late for the bus.
AH HA BA HA!
Oops
throws spoon at toaster
zing

I POP SOME ASPIRIN IN MY MOUTH AND LEAVE BEFORE THE ENTIRE KITCHEN EXPLODES.
Bye, guys.
Bye, babe.
SHRIEEK!
I WALK SUPER SLOWLY TO THE BUS STOP. I'M NOT READY FOR THIS.

NOPE. I WAS WRONG.
I'M *REALLY* NOT READY FOR THIS.

JAIME

I finally pick out an outfit and change quickly. The house is super quiet when I come downstairs. My mom is probably already in her office working.

My brother can be really quiet too. He likes to read while eating breakfast. Or he plugs in some earbuds and watches a science program on the family tablet.

My dad is already gone. He's in sales and usually gets up early to travel. My parents are total workaholics, but they're also complete opposites. My dad drives to different cities around the state all week (selling computer parts or robot parts or something to companies), and my mom works at home as a freelance journalist. Once in a while, she travels too, but usually she just interviews people over video chat.

I remember seeing this one viral YouTube video where some kids burst in on their dad doing a big national interview. My mom's job is like that, only local. She once forgot to button her nursing top when my brother was a baby, and an entire boardroom saw more than just her pj bottoms!

My dad likes to tell that story a lot.

I ignore my brother while I grab some breakfast and scarf it down.

Usually the quiet creeps me out. I like noise. And conversation. But today I need to think about how to talk to Maya. So for once I savor the silence and form a plan while Davey chews the grits Mom made and listens to Bill Nye drone on about the planets.

I kick him under the table. Hard. He just snorts and squishes his earbuds back in.

My brother and I are opposites, too. He's a total nerd, the top of his fifth-grade class. He's really into aerospace. His room looks like a science-fiction set. All his friends are nerdy, too ("adorkable," Maya calls them). Davey actually has a crush on Maya. Every time she comes over, he tries to seduce her with his handmade space-shuttle models.

It's not pretty.

I'm a little more . . . let's say **social.** Maya and I have a reputation at school. Other kids call us "Gossip Girls." I hate that name. We **may** occasionally talk about other people, but we **never** start rumors.

Well, except for fifth grade, when we started one about Joe Lungo having a massive crush on the crossing guard, Mrs.

Dinks. But Joe deserved it. He had spread his peanut butter and marshmallow Fluff sandwich all over our bus seat that morning. Everyone called us "Fluff Duff" until our parents brought extra pants to school.

The point is: we talk a lot. Usually we talk **over** each other.

Also, we can't help but add our two (or two hundred) cents to anything going on around us. Maya and I get called out by teachers all the time. We were put in detention once. We've had notes written to our parents. The only things that keep us from getting into real trouble are that, in between the talking, we pay attention and get decent grades.

I'd actually like to shed that "Gossip Girl" label next year. I'm aiming for a **mature** reputation in eighth grade.

I'm not hungry anymore. I pour the rest of my grits down the drain, which my parents can't stand. What they can't see can't hurt 'em. Truth is I'm too busy worrying about my friendship situation to think about food waste. I'm also a little too nervous to eat much.

Then I think about this one incident from last month. It turned out to be a big misunderstanding. But it still hurts a little.

What the heck?? I'm on SnapGab, and there's a picture of everyone at Celia's except me! Why wasn't I invited?

I don't know, honey. Did you ask them?

Turned out Celia thought I had family plans that night so she didn't bother to invite me. I **didn't** have family plans and I would've **liked** an invite, anyway. Maya reassured me it was all a huge mistake.

I tried to forget about it, but even now it still stings.

Yeah. I should talk to Maya.

I race out the door, not really having formed any kind of plan but deciding to wing it. After all, what's the harm in talking? It's just Maya.

She's my best friend . . .

. . . right?

Maya

I SEE JAIME AT THE BUS STOP AND WISH I COULD TURN AROUND AND RUN HOME. SUDDENLY I MISS LILY'S SHRIEKS.
Hey
Hey
WHO KNEW ACTING NORMALLY COULD BE SUCH A CHORE?
awkward silence
Hey, so...
Yeah?
fuss

BEFORE SHE CAN SAY ANYTHING, THE BUS PULLS UP.
seems to apparate, like in Harry Potter
POOF
WE GET ON AND FIND OUR USUAL SEATS. PERFECT TIME TO TALK TO HER. WE'VE GOT A GOOD FIFTEEN MINUTES.
(bus noise prevents eavesdropping)
wrrrr vrmm
mouth feels super-glued shut
bumpa
bumpa
bumpa

JAI STARTS TO SAY SOMETHING, THEN STOPS. THEN STARTS AGAIN.
You still going to the pool?
Uh-huh.
TELL HER, YOU CHICKEN. IT'S FOR THE BEST.
Hey, M...can I ask you something?
Okay.
Umm...
Yeah?
...well...
Yeah?
...
bumpa
bumpa

HER HESITATION ANNOYS ME. I KNOW, I KNOW, IRONY.
Jai, stop being so dramatic and spit it out.
our English teacher Mrs. Winn's "Word of the Week"
Fizz
JAIME TAKES A DEEP BREATH.
Okay... So, um, I know I've brought this up before, but what's going on? You've been acting weird. Celia and Grace, too.

I PLAY INNOCENT.

What are you talking about?

Like... sometimes I feel like you guys don't want to be friends with me anymore.

That's crazy.

Well, I dunno, that's how I feel. Did I do something to make you mad?

No.

bumpa boing bumpy

Does Celia hate me?
No!
Does Grace? Do you?
Jai, stop it. No one hates you.
Then why—
I SAID STOP IT ALREADY!! THIS IS SO ANNOY-ING!

JAIME GOES SILENT. I FEEL LIKE GARBAGE.
or that layer of garbage that sticks to the bottom of garbage
AT THE SAME TIME, THIS IS SO FRIGGIN' TYPICAL OF HER. SHE JUST DOESN'T *SEE*. I WISH SHE'D GET A CLUE THAT WE'VE CHANGED AND SHE HASN'T.
blah blah
going on about ancient Vines and volleyball stuff
yawn
eye-roll

WE GAVE HER SO MANY CHANCES AND HINTS TO GET WITH IT, OR — WELL, NOW IT'S COME TO THIS.
sigh
bumpa bumpa bumpa
OKAY NOW. DO IT NOW.
Sorry, Jai.
Listen, I need to—
What?
blinking back tears

now feeling like the bugs that crawl on the stuff that sticks to the bottom of garbage

Never mind.
zzz
CHICKEN!

JAIME

I tried. Really tried talking to Maya. It didn't help that I couldn't get my words out. It's weird: usually we can talk about anything. But she's been so distant, it's like a huge wall went up between us.

First, I tried at the bus stop. But then the bus pulled up, and there's no way you can talk when that happens. I mean, it **careens.** I don't know how our driver still has a job; he'd be perfect for a remake of the movie **Speed**. People have to hold on to each other every time he goes around a corner.

Then I tried on our way to school. That didn't work either. "The Wall" was practically to the ceiling. Plus, I was getting carsick.

All I did was make her mad. Which made her yell. Which made **me** upset.

So now I don't know what to do.

Maybe we just need a break. My mom says friends like us, who are joined at the hip, sometimes get annoyed with each other and need some space—just like sisters or couples. I mean, I'm not really feeling that way, but maybe she is.

We (miraculously) make it to school, so I guess we **will** go our separate ways. At least for a couple minutes. Maya heads to the bathroom to put on some gunky makeup (ick), and I go to homeroom to sit and wait to clean out our lockers.

In my head, I go over what happened on the bus. I try to think of what I did that could've made her mad. Or what might be going on with **her**. The only thing that's really changed about our friendship is Celia.

Maya, Celia, and Grace make up my friend group. Maya and I are on the same middle school team—have been since last year. (Our school is so big, each grade gets divided into groups or "teams.") Being on the same team made us even closer than we were in elementary school.

Celia and Grace are on Team "Supersonic" (which, by the way, is a much cooler name than ours).

Grace is the quietest of us, which isn't saying much. She's really tiny, really agreeable, and really giggly. (We've told her to rein in the giggling thing, but it never works.) Somehow Grace knows everybody's business (I think it's 'cause people tend to forget she's there), so she always has the juiciest news. She keeps it all in the group, though.

Celia is definitely the coolest of us. She's the best dresser, has the best music, totally keeps calm in high-stress situations (hello, math test!!), and pretty much likes to take control of everything.

She also has this strange hypnotizing quality (my dad calls it "charisma"; my mom calls it "sorcery") that won us over when we met her in sixth grade. She was from another elementary school but just clicked with us on our first day. Her best friend had gone to private school, so we took Celia in. Or, now that I think about it, maybe she took **us** in.

Even though the four of us don't all have the same classes, we eat lunch together. And have sleepovers and stuff. Usually it's pretty fun. But lately, Celia and Maya have been getting tighter.

There's something else too. When Cee came back after summer break last year, she had changed. She kinda developed a little. Also, she had gone to sleepaway camp and had her first kiss. She wouldn't stop talking about it.

At a sleepover right before school started, she told us about that kiss in detail, as well as some stuff she learned from the older kids. Maya and Grace were curious and had so many questions and couldn't stop giggling.

Me? I was just embarrassed and kinda grossed out.

They teased me that night because I was the only one who was still wearing a training bra and wasn't interested in kissing boys and didn't really want to hear about what those older campers were doing.

All I wanted to do was the usual: give ourselves manicures, eat junk food, watch movies, and talk!

But I was outnumbered.

The rest of our sleepovers were pretty much the same. Maya and Grace would act so eager and dopey around Cee, like she was the center of the coolness universe.

I hate to say this, but whenever Celia is out sick or on vacation with her family, I feel like the three of us have a much better time. It's like the old days when we could talk and talk and just be ourselves.

I miss that feeling sooo much.

Maya

AS SOON AS WE GET TO SCHOOL, I HEAD STRAIGHT TO THE GIRLS' BATHROOM TO PUT ON MY (OUTLAWED) MAKEUP.
not allowed till 9th grade
Mom never notices anyway (probably thinks Lily covers me in peas and ketchup)

I'M SO RELIEVED TO ESCAPE JAIME, EVEN FOR A FEW MINUTES.
(thinks makeup is gross. Seriously?)
Lindsay
body spray

LINDSAY AND I CHAT WHILE I TRY NOT TO CHOKE ON HER FUMES.
takes a good four hours to wear off
ate more beans
cough
telling me relationship woes about Kyle Duncan
flush

I GET A TEXT FROM CELIA.
lets do it b4 the pool

k. will try.
ur the best
blip

I HEAD TO HOMEROOM WITH LINDSAY.
spray either wore off or killed my sense of smell
MR. RYAN ANNOUNCES IT'S TIME TO CLEAN OUT OUR LOCKERS. WE CAN KEEP OUR LOCKER STUFF IN THE BACK OF THE CLASSROOM UNTIL THREE O'CLOCK.
gulp
looks like a bomb went off in mine

JAIME SNEAKS LOOKS AT ME WHILE I PRETEND TO FOCUS ON CLEANING.
will need another hour at this rate
Hey, M? I'm sorry if I was bugging you on the bus.
It's okay.
So, um, which bathing suit are you wearing to the—?
Hey, Maya.
Oh. Hey, Jaime.
Hey!

Cute top, Maya! So, what's going on?
We were just talking.
Oh yeah? About that "thing"?
What thing?
Nothing. Inside joke.
giggle
Oh. See you at the pool?
Um, yeah, sure.
Cool. I bought a new swimsuit.

It's not like your blue one, is it?
No... it's a yellow bikini. With tiny flowers.
Good. The blue one makes you look like Maya's little sister.
JK. Not that she isn't cute.
giggle
Have a great summer, girls.
You, too, Mrs. D. Oh, love your necklace.
Thanks. It was my mother's.

That thing is hideous, but I want an A in English next year.
hee
snort
clicka click
Okay, well, we have to get going. Later?
looking pointedly
Yeah. Later.
CELIA AND GRACE HEAD TO CLASS. JAI JUST STANDS THERE, LOOKING BEATEN AND PATHETIC.
part of me wants to slap her
other part wants to hug her

THE BELL RINGS AND WE GRAB OUR STUFF TO TAKE BACK TO CLASS.
Ready?
sure.
brought paper bags (smart)
not so smart
JAIME LOOKS SO SAD. FOR A MINUTE, I'M MAD AT CELIA FOR MAKING ME DO THIS.
SEEMS LIKE ANY TIME I START TO FEEL THAT WAY, THOUGH, I GET SIGN FROM ABOVE. OR FROM CEE.
ur the only one we trust ♥ ♥ ♥

WHEN SOMEONE LIKE HER TOTALLY TRUSTS YOU, IT MAKES YOU FEEL...WELL...
PUMPED!
YEAH. THIS IS FOR THE GOOD OF THE GROUP. HECK, IT'S FOR JAIME'S OWN GOOD.
I KNOW IT.

I JUST HOPE SHE SEES THAT...
...EVENTUALLY.

JAIME

Maya's acting a little nicer on our way to first period . . . although she's still pretty quiet. Then again, so am I. And upset. And confused. In fact, I think I'm the Frankenstein of feelings.

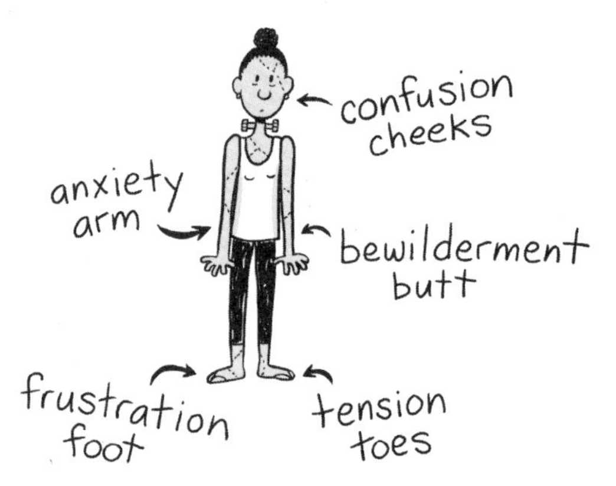

We get to science. Ms. Flancher passes back all our old tests and papers, then gives us free time. I want to try and talk to Maya again. Just as I start to, she turns her back and . . .

What the heck! Is Lindsay her new bff now??

Well, fine. Lindsay smells like a Christmas tree farm, anyway. Let Maya have a sneezing fit. I turn to talk to Anthony Randall instead.

He catches me off guard. Dang. I thought I had my poker face on. I must still be wearing my sad-mad-want-to-rip-off-Maya's-face face.

I smile. **That's** the truth.

I want to vent more, but I'm getting paranoid that Maya will hear. So I change the subject and talk about sports. I'm on the volleyball team and he's on the basketball team. We share the gym and watch each other's games.

Talking to Anthony instantly makes me feel better. Maya glances over. I can't tell what she's thinking.

That's a first.

Maybe she thinks we're talking about **her**. Good. For once, she'll know what it's like. Gotta say, we haven't been this icy to each other since October, when Grace and I accidentally wore the same dress to school and Maya joked that Grace wore it better.

It was around that time that I started wearing padded bras. My mom—who's normally a church lady—caved in after a lot of begging. I remember one morning when I ran out of laundry and couldn't wear one. Let's just say it was kinda noticeable.

My friends couldn't stop laughing, calling me a deflated balloon. I was so humiliated, I almost ran to the bathroom to stuff my shirt with toilet paper. Luckily, Maya had a heavy sweatshirt in her locker, and I wore it all day.

The bell rings. Maya mumbles that she has to use the restroom and bolts out the door. I can't tell if she's just making excuses or what.

I'm so deep in thought that, when someone pokes me in the side, I almost jump out of my skin. Anthony laughs. I punch his shoulder.

We walk out of class together, my heart still pounding.

I laugh a little.

I can see Anthony wants to spit somewhere, but he's finally kicking that gross habit. His mouth puckers into an odd shape, and he stops himself.

Anthony and Nikki Lourde were a "thing" last month. Well, really for like two weeks. My older cousin in California says middle school dating is like dating in dog years. Two weeks feels like two years. That must be true because Anthony looks like his wife of half a century just died.

I poke him in the side.

Oops. We probably shouldn't talk about those two. After all, I'm **trying** to be more mature. But one look at each other's faces and we start laughing.

I know it's wrong, but the laughter feels good.

Anthony kicks along a wadded sticky note on the floor and puckers again. It must be taking all his willpower not to spit. I offer him some gum.

Anthony isn't a guy of many words, and lately he's been depressed as all heck . . . but he's sweet. Despite that stupid spitting habit, lots of girls like him. But it took Nikki being grossed out to finally make him stop.

We walk down the hall without talking. With Maya, Celia, and Grace, being so quiet would be weird. But with Anthony, I can just . . . well, be.

Before we separate for our classes, he pokes me in the arm with his elbow. That's his goodbye. I stick my tongue out, and he laughs.

At least I have one person on my side.

FIRST PERIOD. LINDSAY ASKS ME IF I SIGNED UP FOR VOLLEYBALL CAMP, AND WE START TALKING.

I CAN TELL JAIME'S GETTING UPSET. I HAVE TO GET HER ALONE. MAYBE WE CAN TALK ON THE WAY TO GYM.

Ugh, I should just let Cee do it. This was all her idea, anyway.
But I know it's better coming from me. And if I want Cee to be my bff, I can't make her look bad.
Why does Jai have to be this way, anyway? This wouldn't be happening if she'd just act like the rest of us!

THE BELL RINGS, JOLTING ME FROM MY THOUGHTS. TWO MORE CLASSES TO GET THROUGH UNTIL FIELD DAY.
BRRRNNG
never fails to make me jump
I CHICKEN OUT AGAIN. I CAN'T WALK WITH JAIME. I JUST CAN'T.
Um, I'm going to the restroom. See ya at gym?
I GET TO THE GIRLS' BATHROOM. IT'S PACKED. GOOD THING I'M SHORT.
easier to weave my way to mirror
Ugh, Mrs. Winn totally dress-coded me. I had to roll down my shorts. But I rolled 'em up again as soon as I got away.

That's stupid. They look fine! Ally Davis's shorts are way higher than yours.
I know! The only reason Ally Davis can get away with it is 'cause her dad is superintendent and all the teachers are too scared to say anything.
creak
Ally Davis
SLAM
giggle

whispering
Hey, Cee?
Yeah?
Maybe ...um...
You're not gonna chicken out, are you?
No...
Good. Let's do it before lunch.
I thought you said the pool...?
Yeah, but it's better if it's before lunch. Otherwise... so awkward, right?
Yeah. Okay.

SHE GIVES ME A SUPER HARD HUG.
You're the best, M.
That's why I love ya.
squeeeeeze
M. THAT'S JAIME'S NICKNAME FOR ME. THIS IS THE FIRST TIME CELIA'S USED IT.
I HAVE TO ADMIT...
...THAT MAKES ME FEEL PRETTY COOL.

JAIME

So if Maya's gonna avoid me, I'll do the same. It's not hard—we're just watching a dumb movie, anyway, while Coach Durdle sets up some nets outside for Field Day.

After the movie (well, half a movie, since gym is only forty-five minutes), I change quickly and head to French class. It's now pretty clear to everyone else that Maya and I aren't talking to each other.

I know the reason I'm mad at Maya, but I have no idea what her deal is. Whatever it is, Celia is so obviously controlling it.

I think, **When did this whole mess start, really?**

It must've been right after Christmas break. I was in California with my family, visiting my uncle and cousins. When I got back to school, Celia started making not-so-secret little comments behind my back. "Not-so-secret" because she knows our other friends are talkers.

Then later, she started making the same kind of comments to my face. Stuff like how, appearance-wise, I was "stuck in fifth grade" and "how **retro**" it was that I still wasn't interested in kissing boys. I'd get a little mad, and she would say, "Just kidding. It's fun to mess with you."

In the beginning, Maya would defend me, but eventually she stopped. And started to repeat whatever Celia was telling her.

Then around spring break, Maya and Grace started getting worse. They wouldn't always laugh at my jokes (and Grace laughs at **everything**), or they'd make a comment about my clothes or body or something. It sounded like playful teasing . . . but maybe it wasn't?

It'd be bad enough if it wasn't so **constant.** Thinking about all this makes me sad and angry at once. So much so, that I have what my mom calls an "Aha Moment"* (*Stolen from Oprah).

I decide it's time to just come right out and ask what's going on. Maya owes me that!

It sure takes a long time for her to answer.

Maya

YEP, JAI IS REALLY MAD. SHE STORMED OUT OF THE GYM LOCKER ROOM WITHOUT WAITING FOR ME.

GUESS I DESERVE THAT. BUT STILL, HOW IMMATURE! JUST 'CAUSE I'M DOING IT DOESN'T MEAN SHE SHOULD.
Now I'm mad that she's mad that I'm mad... okay, I'm dizzy.
THIRD-PERIOD SPANISH. JAIME HAS FRENCH. IT'S THE ONLY CLASS WHEN WE'RE NOT TOGETHER. BUT CELIA AND GRACE ARE HERE.
dreading this 'cause I know what's in store
JUST LIKE IN THE FIRST TWO PERIODS, SEÑORA QUELL GIVES US FREE TIME. I THINK OUR TEACHERS' BRAINS ARE ALREADY ON SUMMER BREAK.
¡Bienvenidos! a la clase de español
Just sit quietly, class.

I PLOP IN MY CHAIR WHILE CELIA AND GRACE GLARE AT ME.
VZZZZZ
eyeballs like question marks
Well?
ok, m, this has gone on 2 long. whats with u???!!!?
I STARE AT THE SCREEN FOREVER.

I SWALLOW AND SHOW THE TEXT TO CEE. SHE RAISES HER EYEBROWS.
then gives me "the look"
I TAKE A DEEP, NERVOUS BREATH. DREAD WASHES OVER ME.
NOW OR NEVER.
tappy tap
I START TO TEXT.
ONCE I START, I CAN'T STOP. IT'S LIKE MY FINGERS ARE POSSESSED.
tap tap tak click

CEE AND GRACE LOOK OVER MY SHOULDER. EVEN THEY'RE AMAZED.
clicky click tak tap
jaws dropped to floor
Okay. I did it.
Whoa.
Truth? I didn't know you had it in you.
Tell me about it.

JAIME

My phone vibrates. I make sure Madame Zukosky doesn't notice. She doesn't. Her head is in a book. And on closer look . . . she has earbuds in. Yep, every teacher has tuned out for the summer.

I look down at my messages. Holy tomatoes. Maya texted back a whole essay.

Excuse me. What?

Is this a joke?

First of all, kids don't have meetings. Parents have meetings. Teachers have meetings.

Keeping me in the group? I helped **make** the group. What is going on? This has to be a joke.

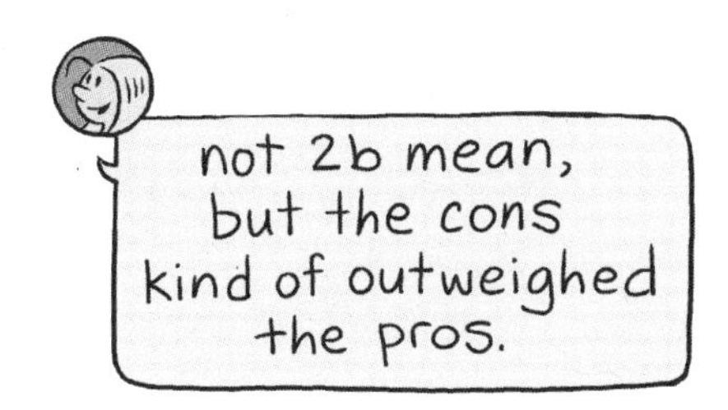

BOOM. There it was. (And by the way, "not to be" means you **are** being.)

No, it's not a joke. I felt this coming. It was stupid of me to blow off the weirdness and tension this whole time.

But it still feels like a punch in the stomach. From a giant. With fists the size of Hondas.

My mind is scrambling. I have a million questions in my head. But they're getting all jumbled up 'cause I'm panicking at the same time.

I try what my dad always says to do when you're panicked or angry: inhale. Count to eight. (Yeah, I don't know why it's eight and not a round number like ten.) Then exhale slowly.

I do it.

It helps. Sort of.

I do it again.

Then it finally hits home.

OMG. My friends are . . .

. . . dumping me!

Maya

I WAIT FOR MORE QUESTIONS, BUT MY PHONE'S GONE DARK.

MY FINGERS TYPE BEFORE I CAN STOP THEM.
click
tap
tak
all. we dont have anything in common anymr. u knew that.
no, i didnt.
NOW I'M JUST IRRITATED. OF COURSE SHE DID. WAS SHE *CLUELESS?* SHE DIDN'T WANT TO DO ANYTHING CELIA—I MEAN WE—DID.
doesn't dress or act like us
doesn't care as much about SnapGab
yawn
neon tee
loud leggings
nekked face
doesn't care about makeup or boys (except Anthony, who doesn't count)
doesn't even care that she doesn't care
Jai doing Jai

I PAUSE. I'VE GOTTA DO THIS. AN' IT'S GONNA BE HARSH. I LOOK AT CEE, WHO NODS ENCOURAGINGLY. *RIP OFF THE BAND-AID.*

so like i said, we listed all pros and cons of staying friends...

pros: u give good manicures. u have the nicest house. u have a nice little bro. ur good at volleyball. ur cute & fun-loving.

cons...

I PAUSE AGAIN. DO IT.
we don't have enough in common anymr. u would rather hang out with anthony than us. u still like little kid movies & tv. u talk 2 much. ur a goody-goody.
we grew up, Jai, u didnt.
MY PHONE GOES DARK AGAIN.

JAIME

I stare at my phone.

There it is. Everything I worried about but hoped wasn't true. In a text. I'm in such shock, I can't even cry. Funny—I think my body is starting to go through all that fight-or-flight stuff, but from the outside, you probably can't tell.

The bell rings. Madame Zukosky rips out her earbuds and shouts above the din.

The class ignores her and makes a mad dash for the door. Geez, it's just lunch.

OMG, lunch. Who am I going to sit with now? I think I'm frozen to this chair.

Madame Zukosky finally looks up and notices me.

My voice breaks on "yeah."

Madame Z rushes to me.

For once, I'm at a loss for words. I can't speak at all. Even Madame Z looks shocked at my lack of verbiage.* (*a Mrs. Winn "Word of the Week")

I'm so grateful, I become even more speechless. I like Madame Zukosky. She's new to the school this semester. Took over after Mr. Drake, the last French teacher (who was about a hundred years old and smelled it), decided to up and move to Arizona.

Madame Z is one of the few teachers who didn't care if I talked in the beginning of class. She let us get away with a lot as long as we kept our grades up.

I cry harder, and snot comes out. Attractive. She offers me a tissue.

After a few minutes, I start to calm down. I blow my nose.

She gets a weird look on her face.

I smile, a little.

I snort and cough at the same time. (snough?)

She smiles sadly and grabs an unopened water bottle from her desk.

She hands it to me, and I open it. I take a long swig. She's right; I didn't realize how thirsty I was. I gulp down half the bottle.

I thank her again and take a small sip.

I'm now counting on my fingers the people I can trust at school.

That's **two.**

Maya
You did it. You're way braver than I thought.
squeeze
MY HORRIBLE FEELINGS WASH AWAY. I'VE NEVER REALLY BEEN BRAVE AT *ANYTHING*.
brave at volleyball
THWUNK
brave at fashion
brave at... well, everything

YEAH, THIS WAS ABSOLUTELY THE RIGHT THING TO DO.
I'm totally craving lunch. Let's go.
SUDDENLY MY STOMACH FEELS LIKE IT'S TURNING INSIDE OUT.
Ungh. I'll catch up. I need to use the restroom.
MINE! My mom packed me a cranberry bran bar!

I FEEL SICK. WHAT'S HAPPENING?
feel like tossing my cookies ~ or my banana muffin
MY HEART IS BEATING SUPER FAST, TOO.
gasping a little
What is this, a heart attack?
Hey, blond girl, you having a panic attack or something?

A PANIC ATTACK. THAT'S IT! I'M HAVING A PANIC ATTACK! WEIRDLY, KNOWING THAT MAKES ME STOP PANICKING A LITTLE.
I'm okay.
breathing and heartbeat slowing down
Good. I need a calm environment.
STILL...
churn
Hey, can you turn that thing down?
...IF I DID THE RIGHT THING, WHY AM I PANICKING?

JAIME

I stay in Madame Zukosky's class for a bit. Just sitting here quietly makes me feel a little better. Once in a while, Madame Z throws me a slight smile. It's sympathetic but not full of pity or anything.

I guess I can't stay here forever. Finally, reluctantly, I stand up.

I start to leave, then pause.

I think about it. Of course she would've. A person really can't be friendless forever, unless she is a total social pariah or a serial killer or something.

I straighten up. From now on, I'm gonna ignore Maya, Celia, and Grace. I'll hang out with Anthony and Tyler. I can have other friends!

She gives my shoulder a little squeeze and I leave for homeroom. We're supposed to hang out there until the bell rings for lunch/Field Day. I can't imagine anything I want to do less.

Except see **her.**

Well, I won't let her see how much she's hurt me. If there's one thing I have left, it's my dignity.

Maya and a few other kids rush over.

I snap.

The other kids look at one another: Kyle; Lindsay; even that quiet girl, Emmie; and that smart girl, Brianna. All the students with last names starting with D. Mine is Daniels. Maya has an H name, but she was D last year. Her parents went through a bad divorce, and her mom decided to hyphenate Maya and Lily's last name to Hilliard-Davidson. Yeah, that wasn't confusing at all. Anyway, Maya begged to stay in our homeroom. It worked.

Now I wish it hadn't.

She gives me a really sad look. It's probably pity.

The others watch me get up, looking weirded out. I'm sure there will be talk.

So much for my dignity.

Maya

I'VE GOT THE RESTROOM TO MYSELF. BEAN GIRL JUST LEFT.

Anyway, meet you outside.
We'll get you a hot dog.
gurrrgle
...or maybe just a ginger ale.
AFTER A WHILE, I GET UP AND WALK TO HOMEROOM.
more hopeful
Cee is right. I did Jaime a favor. I even feel better.
scritch scritch

BEFORE I CAN THINK, THE WORDS TUMBLE OUT OF MY MOUTH.
Jai! You okay?
Why should You care? Leave me alone.
MY STOMACH STARTS TO HURT AGAIN.
STARTING OVER MAY BE TRICKIER THAN I THOUGHT.

JAIME

The lunch bell rings as I get to my feet. I'm a little shaky, and I don't think it's just from falling. Mr. Ryan asks if I need to see the nurse. Tempting. I could pretend I got a concussion or something and lie on a cot the rest of the afternoon. But since twenty kids saw me land on my stomach, she might have questions.

Once Maya sees I'm okay, she dashes out of the room like there's a rocket pack on her back.

Now I'm just humiliated. I take a deep, shaky breath and count to eight. Better.

Okay, I need to stay tough. Ignoring looks, I head to the field behind the school for our cookout. I remind myself that there are only a few hours left and things really couldn't get any worse.

(note: obvious foreshadowing)

WRONG

I start to panic. Anthony is nowhere to be seen. Neither is Tyler. And I'm not really friends with anyone else. Why didn't I make more friends? Why did I talk about everybody? And why did I assume my group was gonna stick with me through thick, thin, and . . . medium?

I'm **this** close to tears. I can't eat lunch alone, I just can't. I'll be known as a loser **forever.**

Okay, okay, deep breath again.

I'm so startled, I almost fall into the bleachers.

It's Anthony. He's standing there with a hot dog in one hand and a water bottle in the other. I'm so relieved, I want to hug him. I don't, though. He might confuse my relief with insanity.

Great. Now I'm school-wide entertainment.

Anthony starts to spit and stops. He sips his water instead.

I wish I knew. It can't just be because I'm not "mature" and "we don't have anything in common." I don't buy it. I feel my cheeks get hot.

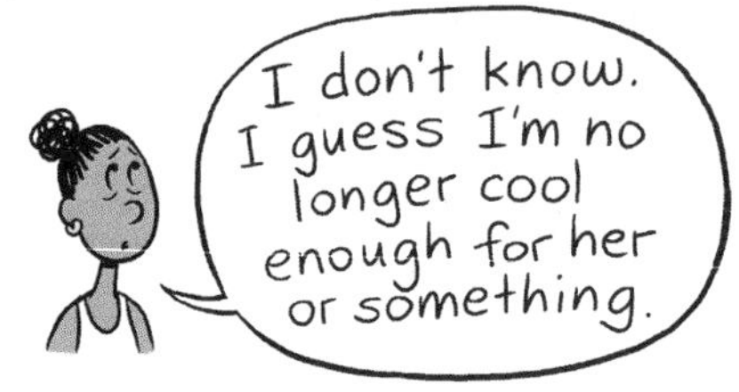

Anthony looks genuinely surprised.

That's the nicest thing anyone's said to me, like, in months. All I've heard lately is what's wrong with me. Anthony's words make me feel like my old cheerful self . . . just for a minute.

We smile at each other. For a split second, I feel something almost like tingles.

I had a crush on Anthony in the beginning of sixth grade. Once we became friends, though, I kind of let it go. He liked Nikki, and then dreamy Zach Finkle asked me out. Zach and I "dated" for a whole month, which—according to my cousin—is like four years in middle school time (Fun Fact: sixth-grade dating is basically just walking the halls together).

OMG! Why am I thinking about that ancient crush? I have more important things to worry about.

Anthony takes a long swig of water and avoids my eyes.

I quickly grab a hot dog and water. We head farther down the bleachers, where I see Tyler sitting with Emmie, Sarah, and Brianna. I don't know the girls too well. I guess Maya and I were always too busy talking among ourselves to notice them much. I did only twice: 1. When Emmie wrote a crazy love letter to Tyler (which turned out to be a joke) and the whole school found out about it; and 2. When Brianna performed in the talent show (up until then, I rarely even **saw** her outside the library).

Okay, **maybe** I talked about that note thing at the time. But heck, the whole school did!

Oh yeah, and when we found out Brianna's mom forced her to be in the talent show . . . there **may** have been some stuff said about that. But nothing **terrible**.

I feel a little guilty, but I shake it off. Past history.

The girls throw me curious looks. Not hostile, just surprised. I suddenly feel like . . . what's that expression? A fish out of water.

Sarah clears her throat.

That jolts Anthony into action.

Sarah and Emmie shake their heads and smile. I smile back and sit down.

Brianna isn't smiling, but asks politely:

I stare at my uneaten hot dog.

They give me uncomfortable looks, like they wanna ask questions but aren't sure if that's being too nosy.

I feel my eyes water, and I try and blink back the tears. **Not now!** I don't want to cry in front of this group. That would make an awkward situation even . . . awkwarder.

That kinda breaks up the weirdness. The girls laugh a little.

Anthony says loudly, almost making me drop my hot dog (he has **got** to stop that):

We eat and for once I don't say much, just listen. Sarah, Tyler, and Emmie slowly start to talk about the school art show, which was just up in the atrium. I know Emmie is a really good artist; I've seen her stuff. I still get surprised about Tyler, who's also pretty good. He really gets excited when he talks about our winter zentangle project (ugh, I hated that!). Yeah, who knew.

Celia's joked about Tyler's new friendship with this bunch, but watching him, he looks pretty comfortable. In fact, I think he looks more at home with this group than with the basketball team. Course, Tyler could care less about what anyone thinks and would probably be fine being on a desert island by himself.

Strangely, I'm relaxing, just a little. I can tell they think my being there is super weird, but they change the subject to favorite (and not-so-favorite) teachers and try to include me in the conversation. I still don't feel like saying much. My mind keeps going back to The Text.

That makes me want to cry again, but I try and hold it together. I start to wonder (against my will) where Maya and the others are.

Just as I wonder, I look up and there they are—sitting on "our ledge," eating lunch . . .

. . . and looking straight at me.

Maya

I TRY TO STUFF MY FEELINGS DOWN, BUT SEEING JAIME ALONE IN THE MIDDLE OF THE LUNCH CROWD GIVES ME *ALL* THE FEELS.

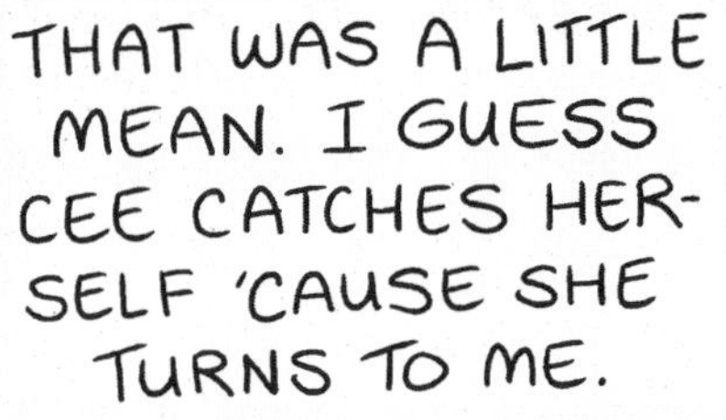

I'M SURE JAI IS MISERABLE, BUT SHE *DOES* LOOK MORE RELAXED SITTING WITH THEM. I TRY TO RELAX, TOO.
So, next year, d'you guys wanna do theme days like we talked about? I vote Monday for Sporty Day. We can wear joggers—
I've gotta admit, though, I don't get it. What does he see in her, anyway?
Who?
Anthony, who else? I thought he had better taste. Then again, he was with Nikki Lourde, so maybe he keeps the bar low.
COULD BE THE HEAT, BUT I'M ANNOYED BY CELIA'S COMMENTS.

I HAVE A SUDDEN, WEIRD THOUGHT.
She isn't...*jealous*...is she?
yawn
Hey, Cee!
smooch
Dude! Did you see that?
NAH!

I'm bored. Let's go do Hula-Hoops.
YESSS!

WE HEAD OVER. THERE ARE ALREADY A BUNCH OF KIDS AND NOT ENOUGH HULA-HOOPS.
That's okay, I'll go play volleyball. Meet you after?
Please. Like we don't know that's what you'd rather do.
(giggle) Total excuse!

IT'S TRUE, BUT I JUST SHRUG AND RUN TOWARD THE NET. BIG MISTAKE.
gulp
cheeks on fire
AWKWARD DOESN'T BEGIN TO DESCRIBE IT.
COACH DURDLE DIVIDES US INTO TWO GROUPS.
Team A here.
tweep
Team B here.
not very original
making sure we're on separate teams

WE START. JAIME'S ONE OF THE BEST PLAYERS, SO THEY LET HER SERVE.
FOOOMP
SOMEHOW, I BUMP IT TO MY TEAMMATE, WHO SPIKES IT OVER THE NET.

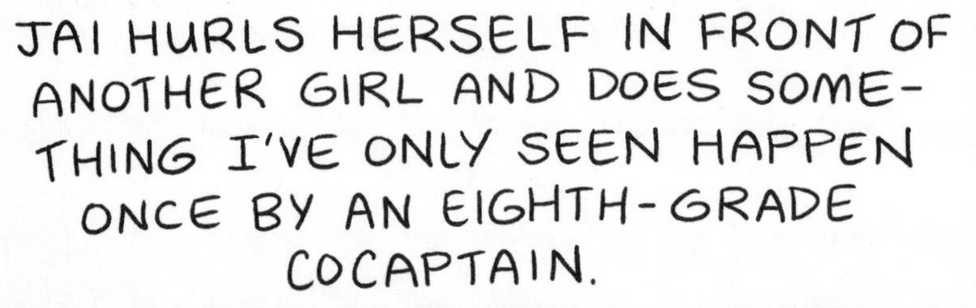
JAI HURLS HERSELF IN FRONT OF ANOTHER GIRL AND DOES SOMETHING I'VE ONLY SEEN HAPPEN ONCE BY AN EIGHTH-GRADE COCAPTAIN.

WOOSH

FWOMP

...A DIVE AND ROLL. IT'S FLIPPIN' SPECTACULAR!
FWOK
EVEN JAIME IS STUNNED. SHE DOESN'T GET UP FOR A MOMENT.
(Ahem) Now if you could do that in a real game, Jaime, that'd be something.

JAIME HOGS THE BALL ON HER SIDE AND TRIES TO DECAPITATE ME WITH IT.
Screeee
Ack!
OKAY, NOW I'M MAD. THAT'S TOTAL SPITE! SOMETHING FIRES UP IN ME, TOO, AND I KEEP DIGGING OR SPIKING IT RIGHT BACK.
FWWPP

FINALLY, COACH DURDLE BLOWS HER WHISTLE AND CALLS THE GAME.
Okay, people, final score: 10 to 7. Good game! Now switch activities. Mr. Bauman is setting up hacky sack on the north end.
Hey, M! We're done. Let's do potato-sack races.
FINE WITH ME! I'M SPITTING MAD AT JAIME FOR TRYING TO KNOCK MY HEAD OFF.

BUT... ALTHOUGH I'M MAD, I TURN TO FIND HER OUT OF HABIT.
anger melting
I SUDDENLY THINK ABOUT HOW WE'VE BEEN INSEPARABLE SINCE KINDERGARTEN.
Haven't stopped talking since we were six...
... till now.
getting impatient
C'mon, M! You'll be my partner.
!

I SURE HOPE THIS IS WORTH IT.

JAIME

I'm ready to hurl knives at my so-called former "friends." Especially Maya and Grace. They're like cowardly robots who do anything Celia says. Maybe I'm not as cool, but at least I'm . . . well, **myself**.

"Queen Cee" may rule with her overlord evil power, but **they** are 100 percent organic, farm-to-table CHICKEN.

I went from sad to steaming mad as soon as I saw Maya at volleyball. All I wanted to do was take her out. I almost did, a few times. But she's no slouch. She's pretty good at the game, especially defense. So we just kept hurling the ball at each other and pretty much forgot that anyone else was there.

Okay, I'd better backtrack. Before volleyball, I was still hanging with Anthony, Tyler, and the three girls.

I liked just sitting there, listening to them talk about teachers, classes, and stuff. I even joined in a little and told them about the time Mrs. Winn made me get up in front of class and read five pages from **King Lear**. I mispronounced every other word, but instead of getting embarrassed, I started mispronouncing 'em worse on purpose and it became a giant game for everyone.

They all laughed. Well, everybody except Brianna. She looked like she wanted to but was holding back for some reason. Maybe she just doesn't have a sense of humor.

Other than that, I was surprised at how much the girls' friendships seemed like Maya's and mine (or how it used to be). Also, I was shocked that Emmie could speak.

But soon, I noticed Celia, Maya, and Grace watching us from the ledge. Then they started whispering. About **me**, obvies.

I tried to ignore them, but Emmie, Brianna, and Sarah started noticing the Loathsome Threesome too . . . and they looked really uncomfortable.* (*The boys were talking to each other and tuned everything out.)

Emmie and Brianna gave me a weird look.

I could see they were growing more uneasy. So was I, but I didn't want them getting caught up in my mess. Besides, it's not like these are girls who enjoy being the center of attention . . . especially **Celia's** attention. Ugh.

Being here was making things worse, so I started to get up and leave.

But Anthony (who finally looked up and noticed) chimed in.

The others quickly agreed. I think they wanted to get away from the Cee-scope.

I decided to distract myself with volleyball. That's one thing that always makes me feel better. As much as I like fashion, manicures, and food . . . I **love** volleyball.

But I managed to turn a fun game into a near massacre.

And now here I sit, having anger-management issues. As if my emotions weren't already all over the place.

Suddenly, I hear Coach Durdle blow her whistle. Mr. Bauman speaks into a megaphone.

Nothing lures a kid (even a big kid) like giant human hamster balls.

The Loathsomes squeal and make a detour from the potato-sack area toward the tumble balls. Which makes me want to avoid that game altogether.

But then I see Tyler and Anthony heading there, and I change my mind. I want to stay tough, and I want everyone to see that I'm not broken!

I get up, wipe my sweaty palms aggressively on my dirty leggings, and head over.

AS WE WANDER TO THE TUMBLE BALL AREA, ALL THE OTHER KIDS WATCH US. PEOPLE *ALWAYS* WATCH CEE.

perfect clothes
perfect hair (blows in breeze with no breeze!)
perfect teeth (no braces!)
perfectly together

GOTTA ADMIT, BEING WITH HER FEELS CELEBRITY-LIKE.

WITH JAIME, I DIDN'T REALLY PAY ATTENTION TO HOW PEOPLE SAW US. IT'S SO DIFFERENT WITH CEE.

snap
paparazzo
click

OKAY, I HATE ADMITTING IT, BUT I LOVE THAT PEOPLE THINK I'M COOL JUST BY BEING WITH CEE.
hand-me-down coolness
AN' SHE'S TAKEN HER STATUS TO A WHOLE NEW LEVEL THIS YEAR. IT'S LIKE SHE'S GOT ALL THIS NEWFOUND CONFIDENCE, AND IT JUST RUBS OFF ON US!
ONLY PROBLEM IS, IF YOU CAN'T KEEP UP...
We had a meeting.
ALSO, BEING WITH CEE COMES WITH SORT OF... A PRICE. LIKE, YOU'VE GOTTA LET GO OF SOME CONTROL. OR OPINIONS. OR—
Grace, we're not twins. Can you stop *walking* like me?

This is gonna be so much fun! Remember last year, when Josh Collins rolled into me on purpose? He pretended he didn't like me, but I could see right through that!
careful my feet aren't lining up with hers
giggle

I REMEMBER THAT TIME. I ALSO REMEMBER THAT JAI TALKED CELIA INTO RACING HIM 'CAUSE CEE LIKED JOSH, TOO. THEY BECAME A COUPLE FOR, LIKE, THREE WEEKS AFTER THAT.
until she got annoyed with all his texts
OMG, okay, you ❤❤❤ me. I get it!
blip

COACH DURDLE AND MR. BAUMAN TRY TO ROUND EVERYBODY UP.
like cattle
tweet
Rah
Form two lines, folks.
moo

CELIA GRABS MY ARM AND LEADS ME RIGHT TO LINE #1. SHE PRACTICALLY SHOVES ME IN FRONT.
You go first and I'll go right after you. You can test the course, M!

I'M THROWN OFF BALANCE. SOMETIMES CEE CAN BE... AGGRESSIVE. BUT SHE'S MY NEW BFF AN' I DON'T WANNA DISAPPOINT HER.
looking deflated, like one of those racing potato sacks
FOR SOME REASON, I SUDDENLY FEEL TORN.
this half proud of celeb status
this half guilty and missing Jai
CAN'T HELP IT. I LOOK FOR HER. HABIT.
Oh.

I CAN'T RACE AGAINST HER. NO WAY.
Cee, can you go first? Please??
So much for brave. But fine.
I FEEL DEFLATED WHEN CEE CALLS ME OUT. BUT THERE'S NO WAY I CAN GO AGAINST JAI.
back to chicken
bok
ESPECIALLY NOW.
if it's possible, even glarier

JAIME

Is it some cosmic joke that out of all the seventh graders, I happen to be standing right next to my stupid ex-bff? My little brother would probably have some scientific explanation for it.

Mr. Bauman raises the megaphone again and goes over the rules.

I can't believe I'm racing Maya! I see her whisper something to Celia, who's standing behind her. Then they trade places.

Seriously?

It feels like the anger is building up in me again, like fiery bubbles in my throat.

Celia and I are first, and the teachers help us into the big goofy balls. Even though we did this at last year's Field Day, I still feel wobbly and unsure getting in.

Celia is screeching and either laughing or crying, I'm not sure. I dream about rolling her like a human bowling ball into Maya and Grace.

I struggle to stand up. I remember last year trying to adjust myself so I wouldn't fall out of the opening. I get myself upright and hold on to the clear, puffy sides. It's kinda slick in here. And humid. I try not to think about that too much. Once we're set, Coach Durdle raises her whistle to her lips. Everyone outside is screaming, cheering us on.

I look over at Celia. I have only one thought in my head.

The teachers give us a little shove, and we're off!

Well, sorta. This thing isn't easy. I slip and tumble right away, rolling to the side of the course. Coach Durdle runs over and reroutes me. I hear everyone laughing, but it's a good laugh, a fun laugh. Somehow I get upright and finally remember how I did it last year: slow, long steps, pressing along the inside of the ball. I also push with my hands. There we go. I'm doing it!

Celia is far ahead of me—what I can see of her, anyway. I can barely see, period! But in a few seconds, I manage to catch up. At first, I think my rage is fueling this thing, but I realize it's just moving too fast, out of my control.

And now I'm veering off again.

Before I know it, I'm tumbling into Celia. Our inflatables collide. That causes mine to bounce in the opposite direction. I slip and fall and toss inside the ball before it comes to a stop.

When it does, I'm laughing so hard, tears roll down my cheeks. This was just what I needed. If I can't beat her, I might as well pound into her! I have no idea where I am. I crawl out, stinking like an old sock.

I look toward the finish line for Celia, but she's not there.

I turn around and see her ball behind me. Celia is sitting on the ground a good distance away from it.

She's all red-faced, like she's about to cry.

I see why.

Her shirt had come off in the inflatable ball. It's a loose top, so it must have flown over her head when we collided. We're supposed to tuck our shirts into our shorts or pants beforehand, but either she didn't listen or it came loose anyway.

Coach Durdle is already hurling herself into the ball and grabbing the shirt. She runs with it toward Celia, who's now sitting and hiding her body with her arms.

I hear the laughter before I see the others. The kids are pointing at Celia, and some of the boys are whistling. Mr. Bauman is trying to calm everyone down by yelling over the megaphone.

It takes only a second for Coach to help Celia get her shirt on. And it was probably only a few seconds of exposure. But it happened. I've gotta hand it to her. Once that shirt is on, she sniffles, wipes her eyes and nose quickly, and gets up without missing a beat.

Everyone claps as she walks back, with Coach Durdle rolling the ball beside her. I pull up behind them, trying not to catch anyone's eye.

Some of the boys (like Joe Lungo and half the swim team) are hooting, and the girls are giggling. I'm no fan of Celia, but I would want to die then and there.

But what does she do?

First, she turns back and gives me the meanest look I've ever seen.

Then she turns to the crowd, smiles widely, and waves. Everyone claps again. She takes a bow.

Coach Durdle and Mr. Bauman face-palm at the same time.

I just stand there with my mouth hanging open.

As usual, Cee steals the day.

Maya

I CAN'T BELIEVE I'M WATCHING MY NEW BFF AND MY EX BFF RACE AGAINST EACH OTHER!
weirdly, not sure who to root for
FINISH

AND EVEN MORE UNBELIEVABLE:
WOO!
clap clap
clap

INSTEAD OF CURLING UP IN A BLUBBERY BALL, CELIA COMES OUT AS THE STAR IN HER OWN PLAY.

I FORGET THAT I WAS TORN. I CAN'T HELP IT.
total awe
That was amazing, Cee! I would've been, like, a wreck.
You turned that disaster around!
I know. No thanks to *her.* Did you see that? She totally crashed into me on purpose.
Actually, I think it was an acc—
CELIA SAYS LOUDLY (BUT OUT OF THE TEACHERS' EARSHOT).
She made it *look* like an accident. But I saw her coming at me like the giant ball from that '80s movie... "Alabama Jones" or something.
giggle
ha ha

Jaime's got jealousy issues.

Actually, it's sad. She should really be more mature.

WAIT. THAT'S TOTALLY UN-FAIR. IT WAS OBVIOUSLY AN ACCIDENT.
psst
psst
giggle
psst
I DON'T SAY ANYTHING, BUT I FEEL MAD... THIS TIME AT CELIA.
feelings getting more fickle than Lindsay Donsky
(meaning very)

JAIME

For English class, we had to read **Gulliver's Travels**. We learned about the Lilliputians, who, as Mrs. Winn put it, were "tiny and insignificant."

After Celia blamed me for the crash, I feel just like that. Or maybe not, 'cause the Lilliputians were still smug. I guess I feel like what would be on the bottom of a Lilliputian's shoe.

I really hate to admit it, but . . .

I **hate** myself for that!

It's funny 'cause only she would be able to cheer me up right now—yet she's the whole reason I need cheering up! Well, she **and** Celia.

I'm so tired, and I know it's not from tumble ball. It's just me.

I smile. Someone gets it.

I pause.

She pats me on my arm and walks back toward the other teachers, who are sitting on the ledge and looking alternatingly hot and bored out of their minds.

Before I have a chance to think about what Madame Z said, I feel a tap on my shoulder, which makes me jump out of my skin. Argh, Anthony!

I turn around, but it's not Anthony; it's Sarah.

I feel a little better.

She says it so shyly, I have to smile. I think about Madame Z's words. **Don't let them get the best of you, Jaime.**

Then I think about how angry I was when I raced Celia. I'm too tired to be angry anymore. Or sad. I just want to forget about everything.

I follow her to the bean-bag toss. Thankfully, it's only the four of us—Emmie, Brianna, Sarah, and me. The rest of the seventh graders are at tumble ball, the sixth graders were called for lunch, and the eighth graders are getting ready for their graduation clap-out.

We toss bean bags for a while, and soon (almost against my will!) I'm kinda . . . sorta . . .

. . . enjoying myself.

I'm seeing these girls differently. Before, all I knew about them was that Emmie was super quiet and artsy, Brianna was brainy, and Sarah was also quiet and had no fashion sense.

We used to wonder why Tyler started hanging out with them.

But now . . .

Maybe this group is seeing **me** differently too. Hope so.

Soon, Sarah says to me:

For a split second, I see Brianna give Sarah a surprised—or annoyed?—look. My thoughts are such a mess today, maybe it's just my imagination.

Her offer is nice, but there's no way. The Loathsomes will be there, and I can't chance that. My stomach drops. Just the thought of them at the pool, whispering about me, making fun of my bathing suit, seeing me fall so far off the social ladder . . .

I look at the three girls and feel ashamed for thinking that.

Still . . .

Oh man, I forgot about the day that Emmie wrote that note, and the entire school knew about it.

Anyway, she's the shyest person I know. So if she could get over something like that . . .

I remember Madame Z's words:

I stop and think.

I don't have to think anymore.

Maya

WE SPEND OUR LAST TEN MINUTES SITTING ON THE LEDGE.
walking back from bean-bag toss
She's definitely better off with them. They all need about ten more years to catch up to us. It would be so funny to send them an anonymous box of training bras!

INSTEAD OF FINDING THAT FUNNY, LIKE I NORMALLY WOULD, I'M GETTING ANNOYED AGAIN.
Can we not talk about them?
Really? You like to talk about everyone else.
Yeah, okay, I just don't wanna talk about them.
Fine, whatever.
CELIA LITERALLY TURNS HER BACK ON ME AND TALKS TO GRACE. WAIT. WHAT'S HAPPENING?
So, Gracie, what are you wearing to the pool?
Oh! I have a new bikini. It's so cute!

THEY CHAT WHILE I MISERABLY THINK ABOUT JAIME. IT'S ONLY BEEN A COUPLE HOURS, BUT IT'S HITTING ME HOW MUCH I MISS HER.
giant club of regret
hit hard
IS BEING FRIENDS WITH CEE WORTH THIS? I DON'T KNOW IF I EVEN *LIKE* HER ANYMORE.
still ignoring me
!!
AN' I CAN'T TALK TO GRACE. SHE'D TELL CEE, AND THEN I'D BE DESTROYED, JUST LIKE JAI.
Then again, she doesn't *look* destroyed.

I THINK ABOUT EVERYTHING I USED TO LIKE ABOUT JAI THAT STARTED TO EMBARRASS ME OVER THE LAST COUPLE MONTHS.
BUT DID IT... REALLY?
Or did it just embarrass me 'cause it embarrassed Cee?
off-key karaoke
giggle!
silly dance moves in gym
giving me wild, funky manicures
ta da!

THE BELL RINGS, AND EVERYONE STARTS WHOOPING AND RUNNING INSIDE TO GET THEIR STUFF.
SEVENTH GRADE NO MORE.
AND I REALIZE: AFTER TODAY...
... I REALLY DON'T KNOW WHAT I WANT FOR EIGHTH.

JAIME

School is done! Good riddance. Walking toward homeroom, I see the eighth graders gathering excitedly for their clap-out. So lucky, escaping this school.

I grab my stuff from homeroom quickly, before Maya shows up.

I get on the bus before Maya does. When she shows up, she sees me and instantly avoids eye contact. She sits with Lindsay, whose body spray has finally worn off.

I sit with some sixth grader I don't know who has the world's hugest backpack.

What a way to end my school year.

I'm no longer mad, sad, embarrassed, or anything. I'm just numb. I guess my body can't handle emotions anymore.

When we get off the bus, I shove earbuds in, turn on my music, and briskly walk the rest of the way home. I don't turn around to see if Maya is there or not.

I start to regret my decision to go to the pool.

At the same time, I'll feel like a coward and total loser if I don't.

I get home. Before I can change my mind about the pool, I race upstairs to change. I say a quick hi to my mom, who's working in the office. Luckily, she's too busy to notice anything's wrong. Some journalism instincts. I ignore my brother as usual. He and his best friend, Alex, are doing science experiments in the kitchen. Nerds.

I gather everything I need for the pool.

I just need money. I head downstairs to my mom's office. I know better than to barge in, even when the door is open. I knock on the door frame. Depending on whether or not she's in deep concentration, she'll either be welcoming or ticked off.

Welcoming.

She digs into her purse and hands me a ten-dollar bill.

She scrutinizes me.

Dang. Journalist's instincts are working after all.

I hesitate. Do I tell her? She's in the middle of a deadline so probably not the best idea. Also, I want to be mature and handle my own stuff. Isn't that what the Loathsomes don't like about me? That I'm not **mature enough**?

I swear she's scrutinizing me again. That look of a journalist who knows how to catch someone in a lie.

Or the look of a worried mom. Sometimes I can't tell the difference. I try to ignore it.

I wave bye just as she gets a phone call. She gives me an exasperated ("Winn" word!) smile and thumbs-up.

I head out but take my time. Everyone will be at the pool by three thirty. I plan to get there a little later so that I'm not waiting around by myself.

The pool is about a ten-minute walk from my house. It's even shorter from Maya's. Dang, why am I thinking about **her**, anyway?

I need an ally.

I text Anthony, careful not to cross the street while I'm at it. Last year some kid from my school got hit by a car doing that. He was okay but had to spend two nights in the hospital. He said getting yelled at by his parents was worse than the broken leg and ribs.

Anthony isn't always so great about texting back right away. I impatiently wait a full four blocks until he responds.

Whew. I have people there. Good people. Real friends. Then why do I feel so jittery all of a sudden?

Maya

I WALK HOME FROM THE BUS STOP, MISERABLE.
I don't even feel like going to the pool anymore.
But I have to, or Cee will replace me with Grace as her bff by the end of the day.
NOOOO!
lugging locker stuff

BUT... I DON'T EVEN KNOW IF I *WANT* TO BE CEE'S BESTIE NOW. THIS DAY IS JUST ONE BIG MESS OF CONFUSION.
Ah ha ha ha!
Celia
giant cauldron of confusion stew
I COME HOME TO CHAOS.
Hey, kiddo. How was your—
WARGHHH
fling

Okay. I'm meeting everybody at the pool in ten minutes.
Who's everybody?
YANK
Cee and Grace.
What about Jaime?
Um... she can't make it.
OW
That's too bad. I haven't seen her in a — arghh, Lily! Dat's my dose!!
cackle!

I TAKE ADVANTAGE AND RUN UPSTAIRS. I'M NOT READY TO TELL MY MOM WHAT HAPPENED.
Still trying to figure it all out
SHRIEK
I CHANGE AND SLATHER ON THREE LAYERS OF SUNSCREEN. I MAY LOVE THE SUN, BUT IT DOESN'T LOVE ME.
SLOSH
turn pink just from a sun-rise
I RELUCTANTLY (FOR MANY REASONS) WALK BACK DOWNSTAIRS.
SCREECH

Um, need some help?
She's beyond help at this point.
(sigh) Go have fun. Enjoy the first day of summer. I'll try not to sell her in the meantime.
thbbbbh
I LEAVE, RELIEVED. I USUALLY WATCH LILY IN THE AFTERNOON WHILE MOM FINISHES HER WORK AT HOME. TODAY I'M OFF THE HOOK FOR THE LAST DAY OF SCHOOL.
Supplies:
polka-dot towel, allowance $, phone, lip balm, giant vat of sunscreen (spf 1000)

JAIME ISN'T HERE, BUT I SEE ANTHONY AND TYLER GOOFING AROUND IN THE POOL. I ALSO SPOT THE GIRLS JAI WAS HANGING OUT WITH EARLIER.
Hi!
Hi, Maya!
Yep, hey, Maya.
SPF

NOT "M."
IS CEE STILL BEING ICY?
soaking up sun
soaking up shade
Oh, that's nice. It's the Island of Misfits again.
(giggle) They sure got tight in, like, a couple hours.

FOR SOMEONE WHO'S A BLABBERMOUTH, I'VE REALLY CLAMMED UP.
Think Anthony will like her once he finds out about all that padding?
giggle
OKAY, THAT'S IT.
We already cut Jai out. You don't have to keep *talking* about her.
It was just a joke. Don't be so *sensitive*, Maya.

THAT'S HOW SHE USED TO TALK TO JAIME A FEW MONTHS AGO.
WHOA, AM I NEXT?

JAIME

At the pool, I look for Sarah, Emmie, and Brianna. I see them sitting way back, by the wall. My ex-friends are in prime spots near the umbrellas. Even at the pool, there's a hierarchy.

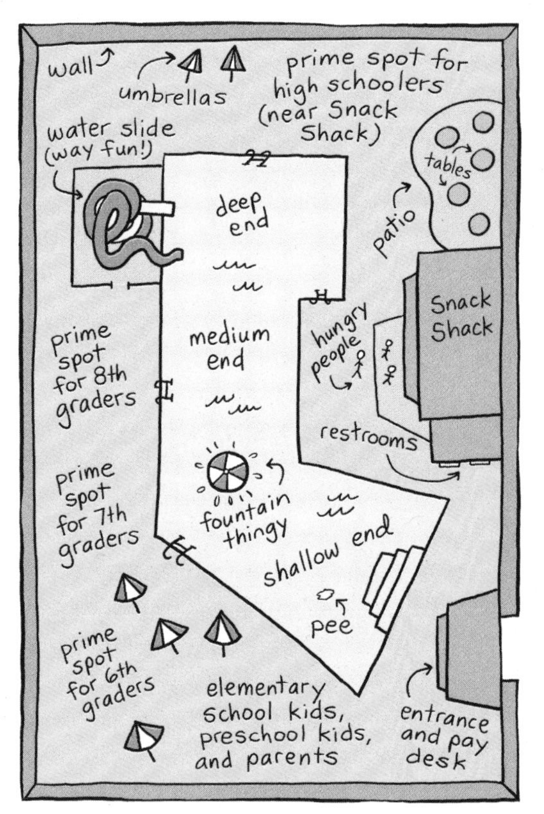

My stomach is still jittery, but I ignore the Loathsome Threesome and head right to the girls, who greet me.

She heads off while I sit with Emmie and Brianna.

She gestures at the Loathsomes.

She's looking at me like I'm some kind of goddess. But she doesn't know that I'm doing everything in my power not to fall apart. I swallow.

Bri throws Emmie an annoyed look. Okay, that was **not** my imagination. I don't know these girls that well so, again, I try to ignore it.

Sarah comes back shortly with the snacks, and soon we're eating the dripping cherry ice pops and I listen while they talk about summer plans. After a while, I even relax and join in.

Except . . . once I start talking, I see that Brianna stops.

What is **up** with her?

After we finish our snacks, the girls lie and sun themselves. I decide to head over to the pool to say hi to Anthony and Tyler, who are fooling around with a water noodle.

He splashes me with about thirty gallons of water. I scream-laugh and jump in. Soon, we're splashing one another and screaming and laughing until the lifeguard whistles and yells at us to quit it. Then she gets down and confiscates the water noodle.

As the towering, over-tanned lifeguard with waaay too much power climbs back into her seat, we laugh and make faces. I'm finally having some fun!

Then I ruin it by accidentally glancing over at the Loathsomes.

Maya looks back kinda sadly.

And Celia glares at me.

For two girls who aren't supposed to care about me anymore, they're sure not acting like it.

Maya

I MISS JAI.
pangs of jealousy

IF IT WERE *US*, WE'D BE IN THE WATER, HAVING SWIM RACES OR JUMPING BADLY (ON PURPOSE... MOSTLY) INTO THE POOL.
mock cannonball
monkey flip

CELIA DOESN'T EVEN WANT TO GO IN THE POOL. SHE JUST WANTS TO LIE HERE AND BE NOTICED.
yawn
(big deal, she's noticed all the time!)
MEANWHILE, JAI IS HAVING FUN AND DOESN'T CARE IF SHE'S NOTICED OR NOT.
Fiiiine. This is boring. Let's go in.
YAY!
FINALLY!
I KNOW SHE JUST WANTS TO GO IN AN' SHOW OFF IN FRONT OF THE (FORMER) EIGHTH-GRADE BOYS, BUT I DON'T CARE.
plop
Yikes
gone from pink to blue

WE FOOL AROUND FOR A BIT, JUST DOING HANDSTANDS AND STUFF.
playing some kind of tag game
paying no attention to us
bump
Oops
Heeey!

UH-OH.
Sorry.
Please. Like you didn't do **THAT** on purpose.
I think that's all in your head.
eye-roll

(laughing inside)

JAIME SWIMS BACK TO THE BOYS AND IGNORES US. GRACE AND I TRY TO DO THE SAME.
Um, let's have a hold-your-breath contest?
k
turning shades of red I've never seen on me
trying to get over awkwardness
AFTER OUR SECOND ROUND, WE COME UP FOR AIR.
Where'd Cee go?
I dunno.
glub

WE LOOK AROUND AND NOTICE HER SWIMMING UNDERWATER, TOWARD JAIME.
IT'S LIKE WATCHING A SHARK CREEP UP ON AN UNSUSPECTING SWIMMER. BUT WORSE.
IT'S HARD TO SEE, BUT I CAN SEE ENOUGH TO KNOW THAT SHE'S...

I GRAB GRACE'S ARM.
THEN I DON'T EVEN THINK.
I SCREAM MY LUNGS OUT.
JAI! LOOK OUT!
JAIME SEES HER IN THE NICK OF TIME, AND KICKS AWAY.
SPLASH

WHAT THE HECK ARE YOU DOING??
I was gonna grab your leg to scare you. It was just a joke.

JAIME LOOKS AT HER LIKE CELIA'S GONE NUTS. MAYBE SHE HAS.
That wasn't my leg.
colder than the pool
It was just to get even with you — for bumping into me before. Now we're even. Don't be so dramatic, Jaime.

JAIME STARTS TO WALK AWAY, BUT TURNS AROUND ONCE MORE.
AND THEN SOMETHING HAPPENS THAT I'LL NEVER FORGET.

JAIME

It happens so fast, it almost feels like it didn't happen at all.

I feel fingers brush my back. At the same time, I feel a light tug on my swimsuit ties. I whip around to find Celia underwater next to me. In a flash, I haul myself out of the pool.

I scream at her, and it's like she's mocking me.

Is she kidding??

That's it. I'm done with these mind games. I just want to tell her off once and for all. But I stop. I do that eight-count thing, just like my dad taught me. It helps, just enough.

Like being in some weird zen state, I calm down. I even start to think this whole thing is ridiculous. I can't argue with Celia. She's beyond it. And she thinks **I'm** the baby.

I start to walk away. But then . . .

I turn around again and crouch down so the others can't hear. They're all staring, anyway.

She doesn't answer, but for a split second, I see it. She glances at Anthony (who's staring slack-jawed at us) through the corner of her eye.

No. Way.

That's when I know talking won't help. And that's when I turn and walk away. For real this time.

Maya

I'VE NEVER BEEN A REAL DEEP THINKER, BUT SUDDENLY EVERYTHING IS CRYSTAL CLEAR TO ME.
I'm going home.
CEE LOOKS TOTALLY UNDONE. DON'T KNOW IF I'VE EVER SEEN HER LOSE HER COOL BEFORE. EVEN WHEN SHE LOST HER SHIRT.
even when Bryan Dean beat her out for "Supreme Supersonic"
Wait, M. You're abandoning me?
I'm not your "M."

CEE TRIES TO GET HER COOL BACK.
C'mon, you don't have to take it personally. This isn't about you, it's about Jaime.
Jaime is my best friend. So it's about both of us.
That's it, then, MAYA. If you leave, don't bother seeing us all summer. And don't text.
FOR A SECOND, I PANIC AND THINK ABOUT TAKING IT ALL BACK. BUT HOW CAN I?
Invisible "truth" glasses"
seeing things clearly
GRACE LOOKS TORN. JUST HOW I FELT AN HOUR AGO.
no more giggling

I HATE LEAVING HER, BUT IF SHE'S STICKING WITH CELIA, I HAVE TO MAKE A CHOICE. THIS TIME I WANNA MAKE THE RIGHT ONE.
Sorry, guys. Bye.
I GATHER MY STUFF AND LEAVE. IT FEELS LIKE THIRTY HUGE, WET WOOL BLANKETS WERE LIFTED OFF MY BODY.
POOL
I WALK HOME WITH MY HEAVY BAG, BUT FEEL LIGHTER THAN I HAVE IN MONTHS.

JAIME

I'm done. I say bye to the others. Sarah and Emmie are sweet and give me a little hug, even though I'm sopping wet. Bri smiles kinda stiffly. She seems torn between liking me and not liking me. I think I get it. I wasn't exactly hanging with her favorite crowd before. I'm sorta surprised that Emmie and Sarah have been so nice.

I'm thankful for that but also sad. Nothing is the same without my best friend. There will be no more Karaoke Nights, no more sleepovers at her house. It's like a piece of me is missing.

Suddenly, Anthony jumps beside me.

OMG, STOP that. I'm already shaky from that whole Celia thing.
Yeah, what'd she try to do, anyway?
Nothing. Doesn't matter. I just wanna go home.
Want me to walk with you?
No thanks. Stay and hang out with Tyler. He looks desperate without you.

He starts to head back but stops and turns around.

I get a little defensive.

My eyes well up.

I laugh.

He pokes me in the arm with his elbow (his goodbye) and jumps back in the pool. Tyler lights up. They start tossing a tennis ball around. I leave them to their bromance.

I start to walk out, thinking about what Anthony just said. It should've made me feel good, but instead it makes me feel kinda . . . sorta . . . what?

Then it hits me.

I race back toward Emmie, Sarah, and Brianna. I'm out of breath.

Listen, I'm so sorry, you guys.
For what?

For... before today. For talking about people behind their backs and stuff. For being a... a...
"Gossip Girl"?

We all look at one another and burst into laughter.
HA HA HA
giggle
HA
borders on crying
eyes rolling to the sky
I hate that name. But yeah. I did that. I wasn't trying to be mean, I just thought it was fun.
Anyway, I really wasn't any better than Celia. *Total* phony.
That's okay, Jaime.
Honestly, I didn't really notice... or care, I guess.

She tells me about the time she overheard this:

And this:

I'm totally mortified, but she smiles. Genuinely, this time.

I feel my eyes well up again. I say goodbye and head out. It's still hot. By the time I get home, I'm practically dry. Except for the tears. So much for my promise to Anthony.

I walk in and go straight past Davey and Alex, who are chugging glasses of something neon green (they like science experiments with food, too). I walk right into my mom's office. I don't care if she's working. I need her.

I startle our cat, Nacho, who's sleeping by the door. He jumps onto her filing cabinet.

At first she's irritated, but then she sees my red eyes.

I break down and tell her all about Celia, Maya, and Grace. I've been bottling up so much all day (heck, all **month**), it's such a relief to let it out. My mom doesn't say much at first. Then she exhales a deep, sad sigh.

Wow. I'm so, so sorry this happened to you, honey. Unfortunately, this is such a common thing at your age.

And let me just say from experience: it feels like the end of the world, but it's not. Not by a long shot.

Ugh. No more "relatable" tales.

Her phone rings.

Best thing she's ever said. I go right into her arms, and she gives me a long, powerful mom-hug. It feels great. After a minute I pull away, sniffling.

Maya
OKAY. I'M GONNA DO THIS.
NOW. BEFORE I CHANGE MY MIND.

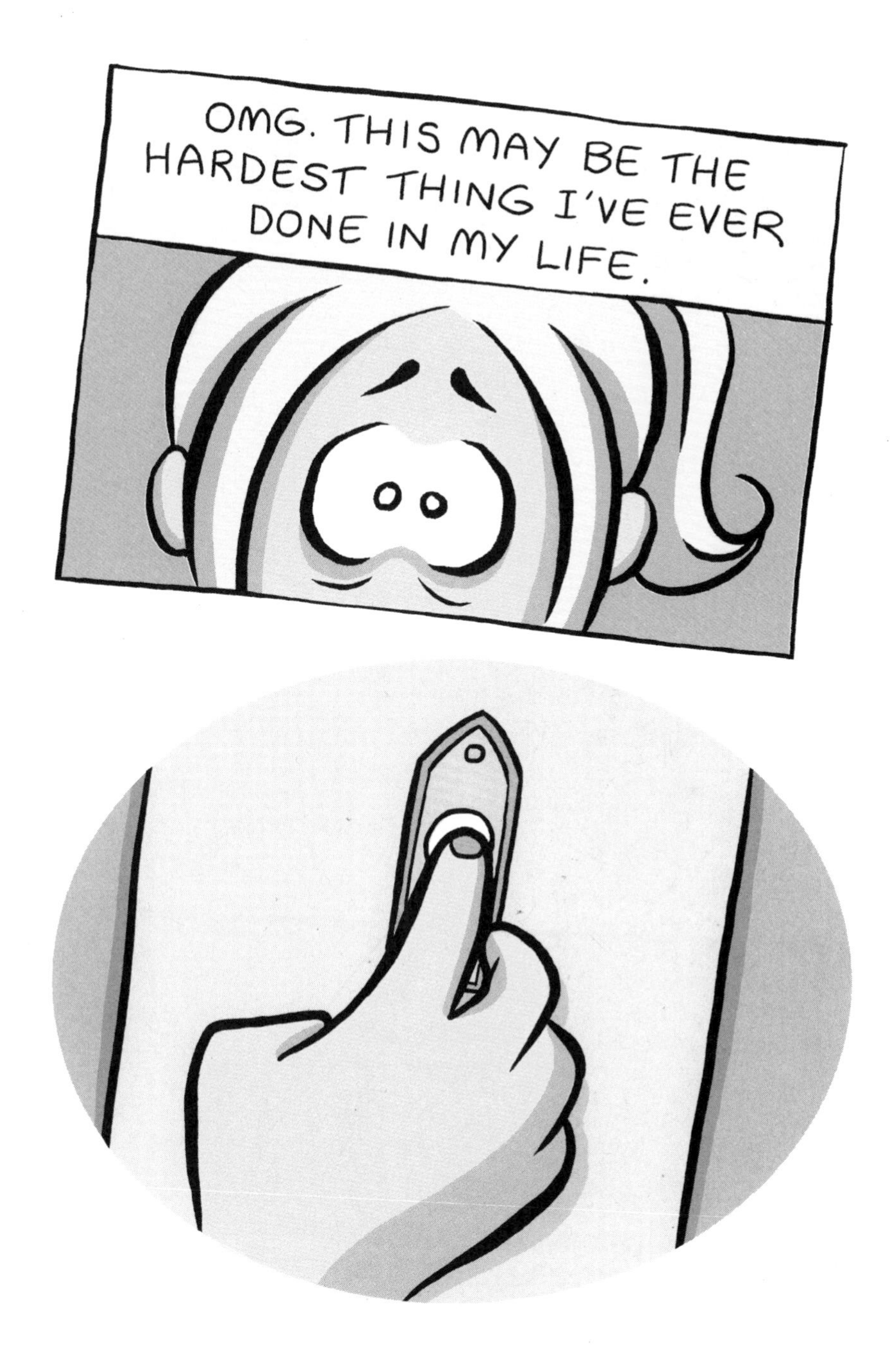
OMG. THIS MAY BE THE HARDEST THING I'VE EVER DONE IN MY LIFE.

JAIME

I sit with my mom for a while. When she's done talking, I feel better. I've even stopped crying.

Dad will be home in a bit. We can go to Ramone's for pizza later. Your favorite.

Maybe.

I leave and close her door. I start to walk upstairs. A nap sounds good.

I almost fall over from shock. What's **she** doing here?

Maya looks really nervous. I hesitate. Do I really want to see her, after everything that's happened? Part of me wants to chew her out and slam the door in her face.

The other part . . .

. . . sigh.

We head up to my room.

I close the door behind us. We sit cross-legged on my (very messy) bed.

She looks really uncomfortable.

We're silent for a while.

More silence. For two girls who usually can't stop talking, we're pretty pathetic.

Maya's eyes get all misty. She finally becomes, well, **Maya** again and spills out her emotions.

I stare at the pile of dirty laundry on my floor.

She starts crying.

She cries harder.

I don't even know what to feel. I'm still so, so mad at her! But underneath . . . I think she's sorry. I even think she didn't want to do what Celia told her to do. To dump me.

But that text . . .

It still hurts . . . a **lot.** I mean, it just happened!

She sniffles.

She sniffles.

For a moment I say nothing. I just draw spiral designs with my finger on my quilt.

We sit in silence again, but I don't even care about the awkwardness. I'm still mad and don't know what to say.

But then I start to think about all the gossiping and meanness and immaturity **I** was part of and didn't even realize. And how it affected other kids.

Emmie, Brianna, and Sarah all forgave me today. Sure, it wasn't the same—we hardly know each other, and I didn't dump them through a text. But I still hurt them. And I hoped—really hoped—these new friends would give me another chance.

We sit quietly for a couple minutes while I think and she waits. Now both of us are drawing finger circles in my quilt.

Finally, I stand up and take a deep breath.

I stare at the gross critter crawling through my laundry. Looks like it built a nest in my camp shirt.

She grins so friggin' gratefully through her tears.

EPILOGUE: JAIME

It's three months later. Weekend before school starts. I'm celebrating the end of summer break with my friends at Ramone's. Best pizza on the planet. We'll be going to Taystee's later, too, for ice cream. I feel sorry for all our family members who'll have to deal with the aftereffects.

If you would've asked me a year ago how this table would be set up, I would've laughed my head off.

So weird, right?

Actually, tonight we're missing Bri; she's at a movie with Dev Devar.

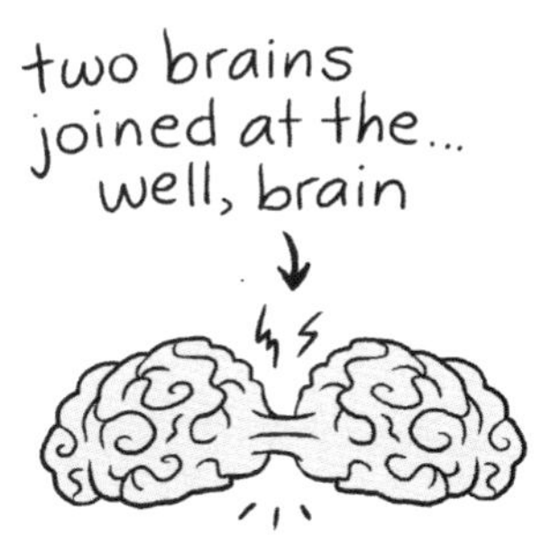

Maya and I are bffs again. It was hard at first (like, **awkward**), but we got through it. Took many, many sleepovers and video dance parties to pull it off. And lots of promises not to break trust again. In fact, Maya was trying so hard to be on my good side, I almost broke it off with **her** (JK)!

In the meantime, we got tighter with Emmie, Bri, and Sarah. For me, especially Sarah. She's kinda quiet until you get to know her, and then BOOM. She can rival **me** with her blabbermouth.

Maya and I don't talk to Grace anymore. That's the only real sad part. She stayed friends with Celia. When Maya and I went to the pool a couple weeks ago, there they were. Seems they formed a new threesome with Lindsay. That explains why M was no longer getting texts from her.

That's another loss, although it probably saved Maya's long-term sense of smell.

Seeing them at the pool made me glad we're no longer a part of that group.

As my older cousin says, middle school is like a huge bowl of drama soup (although I hope to totally prove her wrong **this** year). She was definitely right about one thing: the last three months of seventh grade felt like thirty.

It's funny how you think you'll never get over the worst thing that's ever happened to you . . .

. . . and then you realize that the worst thing that's happened to you can turn out to be . . . well, one of the **best** things.

It may even turn out that you had **another** best friend all along.

(Remind me to thank Nikki Lourde for putting a stop to that spitting thing.)

Madame Z, of all people, walks in. She sees us and waves hello. Tyler shouts, "Bonjour!" and we all laugh.

The kids at our table all yell, "Hi, Mrs. Daniels!" at once. She grins and waves hello.

Am I in trouble?

My mom sits down in a booth across the table from Madame Z, and I sit next to my mom. The server comes to take their drink order while I grow more and more curious.

They look at each other and laugh a little.

Madame Z glances at my mom.
Well, afterward, you got me thinking. Maybe I should try and find my old friend... the one I "ghosted."
It takes me a second.
No WAY!
Way!
She messaged me, apologized, and explained what happened.
I found her on social media through the help of some old high school friends. I wasn't sure if she would, but she forgave me.

The details: they were good friends in high school, then had that falling-out. Madame Z moved out of state for college and then a teaching job.

Fast-forward: Madame Z's kids were grown, and she decided to move back. She got the middle school job when Mr. Drake left. And of course, my mom had only met Mr. Drake—not her—early in the year, during parent-teacher conferences.

In short: one weird, wild coincidence.

I go back to my table, shaking my head in wonder. Soon, I hear the two women chatting and hooting, just like teenage girls. At first, I'm a little embarrassed. But then I smile.

I think about Celia and Grace. Maybe someday one of them will reach out to say sorry. That'd be nice.

If not, I guess that's okay, too.

In the meantime . . .

. . . I don't think I'll worry too much about it.

ACKNOWLEDGMENTS

First and foremost, I must thank two great literary champions: my agent, Dan Lazar, who always has my back and never fails to impress me with his wisdom and kindness. And my editor, Donna Bray, who is equally kind and brilliant, and whose instincts I unwaveringly trust.

So much thanks to Dana Fritts and Laura Mock at HarperCollins, who did a fantastic job of laying out Jaime—no easy feat. It looks amazing.

Endless gratitude to everyone at HarperCollins for their superb skills and talents in the making of these books. I am continually impressed!

More thanks to:

My husband, Michael, who is my greatest cheerleader and supporter. I still don't know how you put up with me when I'm in full work mode . . . which is most of the time.

My kids, Mollie and Nikki, who provide endless material, encouragement, and (when coaxed) feedback.

My friend Mina, who is forced to read my manuscripts. Thank you for managing to enjoy them (and for being generally awesome).

Mom, Aaron, Tina, Brad, and the rest of my family, who have always encouraged me to do this art thing.

And last but not least, to my readers. You make all this hard work totally, completely, and ALWAYS worthwhile.